P9-AGE-713

EARS TO YOUR HEALTH.
www.reshapingtexas.org/kids
RESHAPING TEXAS
A web resource that includes initiatives in Texas, costs, funding sources, success stories and research about preventing and reducing the epidemic of obesity.

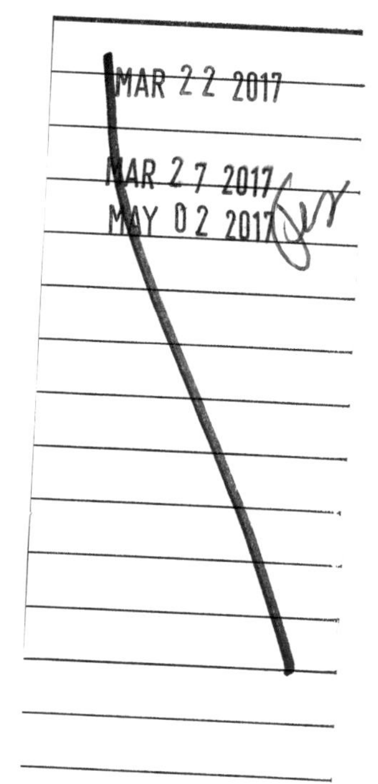
DUE
MAR 22 2017
MAR 27 2017
MAY 02 2017
Cat. No. 23-221

Gregory, the Terrible Eater

by Mitchell Sharmat

illustrated by Jose Aruego and Ariane Dewey

SCHOLASTIC INC.
New York Toronto London Auckland
Sydney Mexico City New Delhi Hong Kong

ISBN-13: 978-0-545-12931-2
ISBN-10: 0-545-12931-1

12 11 13 14/0

Printed in the U.S.A. 40
First Bookshelf edition, October 2009

For Andrew, and the goat who tried to eat his coat

Once there was a goat named Gregory.

Gregory liked to jump from rock to rock, kick his legs into the air, and butt his head against walls.

"I'm an average goat," said Gregory.

But Gregory was not an average goat.

Gregory was a terrible eater.

Every time he sat down to eat with his mother and father, he knew he was in for trouble.

"Would you like a tin can, Gregory?" asked Mother Goat.

"No, thanks," said Gregory.

"How about a nice box, a piece of rug, and a bottle cap?" asked Father Goat.

"Baaaaaa," said Gregory unhappily.

"Well, I think this is a meal fit for a goat," said Mother Goat, as she chewed on an old shoe.

"It certainly is," said Father Goat, as he ate a shirt, buttons and all. "I don't know why you're such a fussy eater, Gregory."

"I'm not fussy," said Gregory. "I just want fruits, vegetables, eggs, fish, bread, and butter. Good stuff like that."

Mother Goat stopped eating the shoe. "Now what kind of food is *that*, Gregory?" she said.

"It's what I like," said Gregory.

"It's revolting," said Father Goat. He wiped his mouth with his napkin.

After Gregory was excused from the table, Father Goat said, "Gregory is such a terrible eater."

"I wonder what's wrong with him," said Mother Goat.

Mother and Father Goat ate their evening newspaper in silence.

The next morning Mother and Father Goat were enjoying a pair of pants and a coat for breakfast.

Gregory came to the table.

"Good morning, Gregory," said Father and Mother Goat.

"Good morning," said Gregory. "May I have some orange juice, cereal, and bananas for breakfast, please."

"Oh, no!" Mother Goat said. "Do have some of this nice coat."

"Take a bite out of these pants," said Father Goat.

"Baaaaaa," said Gregory. And he left the table.

Father Goat threw down his napkin. "That does it!" he said. "Gregory just isn't eating right. We must take him to the doctor."

Father and Mother Goat took Gregory to the doctor.
Dr. Ram was munching on a few pieces of cardboard.

"What seems to be the trouble?" he asked.

"Gregory is a terrible eater," said Mother Goat. "We've offered him the best—shoes, boxes, magazines, tin cans, coats, pants. But all he wants are fruits, vegetables, eggs, fish, orange juice, and other horrible things."

"What do you have to say about all of this, Gregory?" asked Dr. Ram.

"I want what I like," said Gregory.

"Makes sense," said Dr. Ram. He turned to Mother and Father Goat. "I've treated picky eaters before," he said. "They have to develop a taste for good food slowly. Try giving Gregory one new food each day until he eats everything."

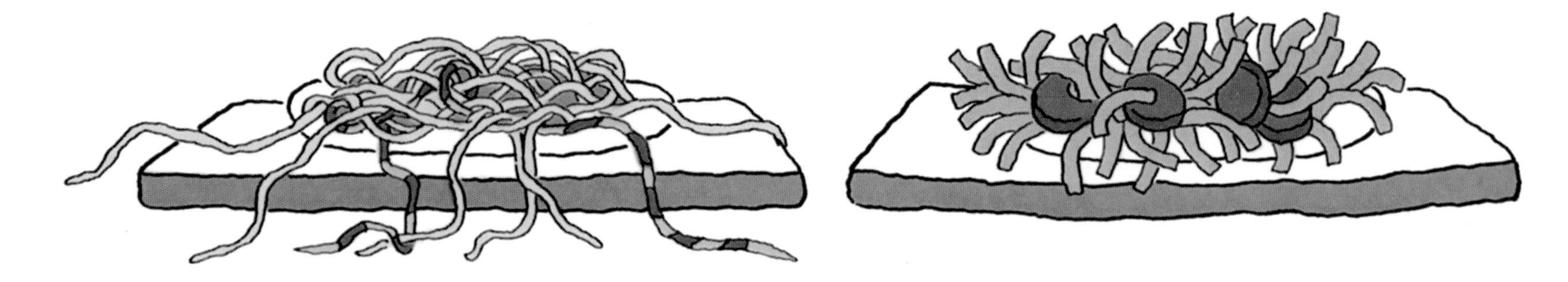

That night for dinner Mother Goat gave Gregory spaghetti and a shoelace in tomato sauce.

"Not too bad," said Gregory.

The next day she gave him string beans and a rubber heel cut into small pieces.

"The meal was good and rubbery," said Gregory.

The day after that, Mother Goat said, "We have your favorite today. Vegetable soup. But there is one condition. You also have to eat the can."

"Okay," said Gregory. "What's for dessert?"

"Ice cream," said Father Goat. "But you have to eat the box, too."

"Yummy," said Gregory.

"I'm proud of you," said Father Goat. "You're beginning to eat like a goat."

"I'm learning to like everything," said Gregory.

One evening Father Goat asked, "Has anyone seen my striped necktie?"

"Not since breakfast," said Mother Goat. "Come to think of it, I haven't seen my sewing basket today. I left it in the living room after supper last night."

Father Goat turned to Gregory. "Gregory, have you been eating between meals?"

"Yes," said Gregory. "I can't help it. Now I like everything."

"Well," said Mother Goat, "it's all right to eat like a goat, but you shouldn't eat like a pig."

"Oh," said Gregory.

After Gregory went to bed, Mother Goat said, "I'm afraid Gregory will eat my clothes hamper."

"Yes, and then my tool kit will be next," said Father Goat. "He's eating too much. We'll have to do something about it."

The next evening, just before supper, Mother and Father Goat went to the town dump.

They brought home eight flat tires, a three-foot piece of barber pole, a broken violin, and half a car. They piled everything in front of Gregory's sandbox.

When Gregory came home for supper he said, "What's all that stuff in the yard?"

"Your supper," said Father Goat.

"It all looks good," said Gregory.

Gregory ate the tires and the violin. Then he slowly ate the barber pole. But when he started in on the car, he said, "I've got a stomachache. I have to lie down."

Gregory went to his room.
"I think Gregory ate too much junk," said Father Goat.
"Let's hope so," said Mother Goat.

All night Gregory tossed and twisted and moaned and groaned.

The next morning he went down for breakfast.

"What would you like for breakfast today, Gregory?" asked Father Goat.

"Scrambled eggs and two pieces of waxed paper and a glass of orange juice," said Gregory.

"That sounds just about right," said Mother Goat.

And it was.